New York Times Best-Selling Authors
Henry Winkler & Lin Oliver

Here's HANK

Fake Snakes and Weird Wizards

ILLUSTRATED BY SCOTT GARRETT

Grosset & Dunlap
An Imprint of Penguin Group (USA) LLC

To my hero, Daniel Silva—a friend and writer
of great adventures. And to Stacey, always—HW

For Tyler, Gregory, and Alex King . . .
childhood and forever friends—LO

For my wonderful Nan, my earliest fan!—SG

GROSSET & DUNLAP
Published by the Penguin Group
Penguin Group (USA) LLC, 375 Hudson Street, New York, New York 10014, USA

USA | Canada | UK | Ireland | Australia | New Zealand | India | South Africa | China

penguin.com
A Penguin Random House Company

Text copyright © 2015 by Henry Winkler and Lin Oliver Productions, Inc.
Illustrations copyright © 2015 by Scott Garrett. All rights reserved.
Published by Grosset & Dunlap, a division of Penguin Young Readers
Group, 345 Hudson Street, New York, New York, 10014.
GROSSET & DUNLAP is a trademark of Penguin
Group (USA) LLC. Printed in the USA.

Typeset in Dyslexie Font B.V.
Dyslexie Font B.V. was designed by Christian Boer.

Library of Congress Cataloging-in-Publication Data is available.

ISBN 978-0-448-48252-1 (pbk)   10 9 8 7 6 5 4 3 2
ISBN 978-0-448-48474-7 (hc)   10 9 8 7 6 5 4 3 2

The books in the Here's Hank series are designed using the font Dyslexie. A Dutch graphic designer and dyslexic, Christian Boer, developed the font specifically for dyslexic readers. It's designed to make letters more distinct from one another and to keep them tied down, so to speak, so that the readers are less likely to flip them in their minds. The letters in the font are also spaced wide apart to make reading them easier.

Dyslexie has characteristics that make it easier for people with dyslexia to distinguish (and not jumble, invert, or flip) individual letters, such as: heavier bottoms (b, d), larger than normal openings (c, e), and longer ascenders and descenders (f, h, p).

This fun-looking font will help all kids—not just those who are dyslexic—read faster, more easily, and with fewer errors. If you want to know more about the Dyslexie font, please visit the site www.dyslexiefont.com.

CHAPTER 1

"Hank!" my sister, Emily, yelled, as she ran up to me and grabbed my arm. "You have to come meet Ginger. She's the cutest snake I've ever seen."

"Emily," I said, "long slimy reptiles with no eyelids or ears are not cute. They're creepy."

"Ginger's not slimy. Her skin is dry. Come pet her."

"I don't pet snakes, or anything else that could eat me whole for lunch."

Our family was spending the morning at the West End Avenue street fair. The whole block was lined with booths selling everything from blueberry muffins to tube socks. Leave it to Emily to find the one snake booth. That girl can sniff out a reptile better than my dog, Cheerio, can sniff out a hunk of pot roast under the dining-room table.

Ignoring Emily, I headed for a booth that was selling cool comic books. Emily stood there and stomped her foot.

"Mom! Dad!" she whined. "This isn't fair. We just spent twenty minutes waiting for Hank to taste every flavor of ice cream when we knew he was going to pick cherry-vanilla all along. Now the family should do something I want to do."

"Emily has a good point, Hank," my mom said. "I think we should all go say hello to Ginger the snake."

"Fine," I muttered. "But I'm not touching her with any part of my body. I will use my eyes and that's it."

We walked over to a large purple sign that read RALPH'S REPTILE SHOW. Under the sign, there was a table with some reptiles displayed in different kinds of glass tanks. A giant tortoise was sitting in the middle of the table. And when I say giant, I mean *giant*. That guy's shell was as big as my bathroom sink. In front of the table was Ralph himself, with a long orange, yellow, and black striped snake wrapped around his arm.

"There's Ginger!" Emily screamed.

"Hi, Emily," Ralph said. "Oh, I see you've brought your family over to meet Ginger."

"They're all so excited to get to know her," Emily said, reaching out to stroke Ginger's long back.

"Make that all but one of us," I added quickly. "I hope this doesn't hurt your feelings, Ralph, but I'm not a big snake petter."

"Well, then maybe I can interest you in Clive, my snow leopard gecko," Ralph said. "Or Boris, my adorable blue-tailed skink."

Okay, I don't even know what a skink is. But it sounds too close to "stink" for me to even consider petting it.

Ralph was wearing a tan floppy

hat that looked like his head had
sweated in it for at least a hundred
years. He had on a brown shirt and
shorts, brown construction boots,
and a shirt with a million pockets
and zippers. Maybe that's where
he keeps his skinks.

"Is that tortoise
even alive?"
I asked Ralph.
"He's not
moving."

"You mean Speedy?" Ralph
petted the tortoise's bumpy head
with two fingers. "He's probably
just thinking about the lettuce leaf
he had for lunch. If you want a
little more excitement, you should
get to know Ginger. She's a hoot."

Ralph moved his arm so that Ginger's face was very close to my nose. Maybe it wasn't *very* close, but it was close enough for me to jump way back.

"Look at Hank," Emily laughed. "Afraid of a little snake."

"I'm not afraid, exactly," I told her. "I just don't happen to love snakes the same way you do. Maybe I'm not an animal person."

"You love Cheerio, don't you?"

"Of course. But Cheerio's a dog, which means you can play ball with him. And take him for a walk. Last time I checked, they don't make leashes for snakes."

"Snakes are very sweet in their own way," Ralph said. "Take Ginger, for instance. She's a mud snake. She loves children. She's a big hit at kids' birthday parties."

"Wow," Emily said. "I wish she could come to mine. It's coming up soon. I already sent out the invitations and everything."

Ralph reached down to the stack of brochures he had on the table and handed my dad one.

"I bring my reptile show to lots of kids' birthday parties," he said. "And I'd be happy to come to Emily's."

"That's a deal!" Emily said. "I'm going to call everyone I've invited and let them know that there's a new theme to my party. Everybody else has a princess dress-up party. Nobody has had snakes before."

"That's because kids don't like attending birthday parties with creatures whose jaws unlock so they can swallow the birthday cake whole," I said.

"I don't care what you think, Hank. It's my party."

"Hold up there, Emily," my dad said, putting the brochure in his coat pocket. "We have a lot to discuss here."

"And we should do that on the way home," my mom said, taking Emily's hand to lead her away from Ralph.

"See you soon," Emily called
out to Ralph. "Tell Ginger I'll
make a special party hat for her."

"We'll have to see about
that," my dad whispered to Ralph.

"I understand," Ralph
answered. "My phone number is
on the brochure. Let me know
as soon as you decide, because

Ginger is a very popular snake."

As we walked up 78th Street to our apartment, Emily didn't stop jabbering for a minute. My dad was just the opposite. He was quiet. His eyebrows were all wrinkled and his mouth was turned down into a frown.

"Look, Emily," my dad said when we reached our building. "I don't want to disappoint you, but we can't have Ralph's Reptile Show at your party. I glanced at the prices, and it's too expensive for us."

Emily stopped in her tracks and so did her mouth.

She stared at my dad like he had just told her the sky was falling.

"But, Daddy," she cried. "I'm only going to turn seven once in my life."

"Well, sweetie," my mom said, "we can still have a nice party for you."

Emily's eyes filled with tears. She pulled open the front door and ran through the hallway to the elevator. I saw her pushing the elevator button like she was hammering a nail with her thumb. I felt sorry for the elevator button, and my mom felt sorry for Emily.

"She wants that party so badly," she whispered to my dad.

"I wish we could afford it," he said. "But we can't."

We rode up the elevator in silence, except for the sound of Emily sniffling. When we got to our apartment, my dad opened the door, and Cheerio came running out to greet us. Even his wagging tail didn't cheer Emily up. As I petted Cheerio, I remembered how Emily had stood up for me when I wanted to keep him, and my dad had said no. Suddenly, I felt something surprising in the pit of my stomach, and it had nothing to do with wanting a pepperoni pizza.

What I wanted was to help my sister. Now, how weird is that?

CHAPTER 2

FIVE WAYS I COULD HELP EMILY ENJOY HER BIRTHDAY

BY HANK ZIPZER

1. I could buy her a black-and-white cookie. (Except it's my favorite cookie in the world, and I'd probably eat it before I got home.)

2. I could buy her a dill pickle. (I'd probably eat that before I got home, too.)

3. I could offer to clean the cage of her iguana, Katherine. (Noooooooooooo, I can't. Just the thought of lizard droppings makes me want to wash my hands for twenty-two hours.)

4. I could dress up as a snake and pretend to be Ginger. (Except my tongue isn't long enough. Also, it's not forked— at least it wasn't the last time I looked.)

5. I could magically produce a snake out of thin air. (Hey . . . now there's an idea. I'll have to talk to Frankie about that.) *

* Frankie is an incredible magician. Once he almost pulled a nickel out of my nose, but I sneezed and blew it out before he could get to it.

CHAPTER 3

As soon as we got into our apartment, Emily ran to her room and slammed the door. I followed her and stood patiently outside of it, knocking until my knuckles hurt. She never said "Come in" or "Go away."

"Emily!" I called. "Open the door. I have a great idea about your party."

"Oh really? And what is your great idea, as if you could have one?"

"Open the door and I'll tell you."

I heard her walking across the carpet, then the door opened a crack.

"What?" she said.

"Well," I began. "You want a snake at your party, right?"

"Duh."

"So all you have to do is produce one out of thin air. Problem solved."

I smiled my best Hank Zipzer smile, giving her a touch of the old Zipzer attitude. It didn't work. She didn't buy it for one minute.

"Hank," she said. "That is the craziest thing you've ever said.

Snakes don't appear out of thin
air. Now stop bugging me."

She started to close the
door, but before she could,
I stuck my foot in the doorway
to block it. I knew I had to come
up with a plan she'd believe.

Unfortunately, I didn't have one. But to my surprise, when I opened my mouth, this is what came out.

"Snakes do appear out of thin air," I said. "If you know the right people. And I do."

"Who?" she asked.

I opened my mouth again, and this time, an even bigger surprise was waiting on my tongue.

"The Westside Wizard," I said. "Don't tell me you've never heard of him. His specialty is pulling snakes out of thin air and twirling them above his head. They get a little dizzy, but they love it because it makes kids happy."

Emily looked at me suspiciously.

"And how do you know this
Westside Wizard?" she asked.
"I've never heard of him."
    "Emily, you may have forgotten,
but I'm in the second grade.

We second-graders know all kinds
of things you little first-graders
don't."

"You don't know how to
subtract, and I do," Emily pointed
out.

"Okay, fine," I told her.
"You can talk about math all
you want. I'll just call the
wizard and tell him you're not
interested in having him come
to your party."

"No, no. Don't do that, Hank.
Do you think he'd really come?
The party's only a week away."

I gave her that Zipzer smile
again.

"He will if I ask him," I said
with confidence. Let me just say

right here, I have no idea where that confidence was coming from. I had never heard of the Westside Wizard. It was just something that fell out of my mouth.

I noticed that Emily was smiling. And it was the same excited smile she'd had at Ralph's booth at the street fair.

"Hank! You are the best big brother in the world."

She reached out and gave me a giant hug. Right in the middle of it, we both realized that this was weird. First of all, we don't hug. And second of all, she grabbed me so suddenly that her braids slapped me in the face.

The hug stopped almost as soon
as it started, which was just fine
with me.

Emily rushed past me and ran
into the living room.

"Where are you going?"
I shouted.

"To call all the friends I

invited and tell them about the Westside Wizard. This is going to be the best birthday party they've ever been to."

On the one hand, it was good to see Emily so excited.

On the other hand, I had gotten myself into a giant pickle. Actually, make that a whole jar of pickles. Who was this Westside Wizard I had just made up? And where was I going to find him? And even if I did find him, how was he going to pull a snake out of thin air?

Those are good questions, I said to myself.

Now all I needed were some good answers.

CHAPTER 4

When I get myself into trouble, there are only two ways out, and their names are Frankie Townsend and Ashley Wong. I can't tell you how many times my two best friends have saved me from disaster. Like the time I spilled glue, and my fingers got so stuck together, I couldn't even pick up a pencil. I thought I was going to have to take my spelling test holding the pencil in my mouth, until Frankie and Ashley pulled me to the sink in the back of the room. I didn't know that soaking your hands in warm water would melt the glue away. Too bad they couldn't take my spelling test for me, because as it turned out, I flunked it.

So as Emily called her friends, my only thought was to call Frankie and Ashley.

"Emergency meeting in the clubhouse," I said into the phone. "Now."

Five minutes later, the three of us were in the basement storage room we call our clubhouse. I started to tell them what happened, talking a mile a minute.

"Wait a minute, Zip," Frankie interrupted. "You told your sister *what*?"

"And you said you knew *who*?" Ashley chimed in.

"You heard me," I told them, trying to appear like I knew what I was doing. "What's the big deal?"

"The big deal," Frankie said, "is that—one—there is no such person as the Westside Wizard."

"And two," Ashley added, "even if he did exist, he couldn't pull a snake out of thin air. No one can."

"But there actually is a Westside Wizard," I explained. "You're looking at him."

I held my arms out and bowed.
Frankie shook his head.

"Uh-oh," Frankie said. "Here
comes one of Hank's totally crazy
plans."

"You know how to pull scarves
out of a top hat, right?" I began.
"You can teach me that trick.
Then all we have to do is tie a
snake to the end of the scarves.
Ba-boom, it's magic."

"Where are we supposed to

get this snake?" Ashley asked.
"In the snake aisle at the
ninety-nine-cent store?"

"Great idea, Ashweena!" I said.
"They actually have rubber snakes
there. We'll go and pick one that
looks really real, like with a forked
tongue and everything."

"Well, even if we do find a
real-looking snake," Ashley said,
"you still have to figure out a way
to look like a wizard. You're not
exactly a Harry Potter lookalike."

"You can help me make a
costume," I said to her. "You're
good at that."

I could see that this idea
interested Ashley. She pushed
her glasses back on her nose and

twirled her ponytail. She does
that when she's thinking.

"Well, you'd need a great
costume so Emily doesn't
recognize you," she said. "A
wizard hat and robe, a big long
beard, and maybe some sunglasses
that cover up most of your face."

"And I can change my voice so
that it sounds all deep and old
and wizardy." I was starting to
love this idea. I switched into my
best wizard voice. "Behold, with
a wave of my arms, I will cast a
powerful spell on you," I growled.

"You sound like a frog with a
cold," Frankie said.

"Okay, maybe my wizard voice
isn't great now, but I can work on

it. I'll study old Mizbam the Mighty cartoons."

Suddenly, Frankie's eyes lit up.

"My big brother Otis went to his sixth-grade Halloween parade as Mizbam the Mighty," he said. "I'll bet my mom packed his costume away in one of these boxes. It would be perfect for you!"

We jumped up and started reading the labels of all the cardboard boxes that lined the shelves of the storage room. Summer clothes. Stuffed animals. Pots and pans. Soccer trophies. Finally, we came to one labeled OTIS. We pulled it down and took off the top. Frankie searched the box, sorting through some baby pictures of Otis.

Then he picked up one and burst out laughing.

"Don't tell Otis," he howled, "but here he is lying on a furry rug, with his naked butt sticking up in the air."

Ashley and I cracked up.

"Oh, here's what we're looking for," Frankie said, reaching way down to the bottom of the carton. He pulled out a pointed hat and a black robe with shiny silver stars. There was even a long white beard made out of cotton balls glued together.

"It's perfect," Ashley said. "Try it on, Hank."

I slipped the robe over my head. Otis is tall, so the robe was very long on me. The arms almost touched the ground. When I slipped the beard around my ears, the end of it went down to my belly button.

"Looks good," Frankie said, "but I still know it's you."

"We need dark glasses," Ashley suggested, "to cover the rest of your face."

She looked over the boxes and found one labeled MRS. FINK'S VACATION ITEMS. Inside, she found a large polka-dot bathing suit, lots of flowered sun hats, and a hot-pink pair of sunglasses covered with rhinestones.

"Oh no, I'm not wearing those," I said.

"Well, you can hope Emily doesn't recognize you," Ashley said with a shrug. "But I think she will, because I can."

"Okay, you win." I took the pink sunglasses from Ashley and put them on.

They worked. With the hat and the robe and the beard and the glasses, you'd never know it was me.

As I strutted around the clubhouse in my new costume, I felt like my plan was off to a good start.

"Now all you have to do is learn the magic trick," Frankie said. "No problem."

That was easy for him to say. Frankie learns everything really fast. But for me, learning new things is hard. I mean really hard.

Don't let yourself think about that now, Hank, I told myself.

But I noticed that myself was too nervous to answer.

CHAPTER 5

We got started right away.
Frankie took the elevator up to
his apartment to get the magic
trick. While he was gone, Ashley
suggested I practice walking
around and talking with my
costume on. I was pretty good
about not tripping on the robe,
but the beard was another story.
Every time I moved my lips,
the beard slipped off my face
and landed on the ground. It
looked like a fluffy white bunny

rabbit fell asleep on my shoes.

"This beard isn't working,"
I told Ashley. "Either it's too big
or my face is too small."

"I don't think your face is going
to grow before the party," Ashley
answered. "So we'll have to come
up with another way to keep the
beard on."

She looked around the storage
room and noticed a roll of clear
packing tape sitting on one of the
shelves.

"Just the thing," she said.

She took the roll of tape and
tore off two small pieces. Then I
held very still while she taped the
beard to both sides of the pink
sunglasses.

"Now your beard won't fall down unless you take the sunglasses off," Ashley said.

By then, Frankie had returned with the magic trick. To me, it just looked like an empty black velvet bag.

"Oh, but feast your eyes on this," Frankie said, turning the bag inside out. "What do you see?"

"An empty bag."

Frankie turned the bag right-side out, so it was back to normal. Then

with a big smile, he reached in
and pulled out a long chain of
colored scarves.

"*Zengawii!*" he said. "It's magic."
"How'd you do that?" I asked.
"Very well." Frankie laughed.
"That's what us magicians always
say when someone asks how we do
a trick."
"Come on, Frankie. You have
to tell me," I said. "How else am
I going to learn?"
"Okay, but you have to promise

not to tell. It's the Magicians' Code. We don't share our secrets."

"I promise."

"Me too," Ashley said.

Frankie lowered his voice to a whisper. "The scarves are in a hidden compartment inside the lining of the bag. When you reach inside, you have to open the Velcro pocket to get to the scarves, without anyone seeing what you're doing. It takes practice. You're going to have to spend a lot of time on this trick, Hankster."

"Okay," I agreed. "But first let's get the snake, and tie it to the end of the scarves.

There's no point in practicing without it. I know right where they are at the ninety-nine-cent store . . . in between the canned artichokes and the Little Tugboat toothbrushes."

"Then what are we waiting for?" Ashley asked.

We took the elevator up to the tenth floor and burst into my apartment. My dad was sitting in his leather chair, doing a crossword puzzle.

"Dad!" I said. "We need to make an emergency trip to the ninety-nine-cent store. Can you please take us?"

My dad didn't look up. He was concentrating.

"What's a seven-letter word for this clue: 'You don't want to bite this in public.'"

"A crossing guard," I answered.

Now my dad looked up. "How did you come up with that, Hank?"

I smiled proudly. "My brain is on fire, Dad."

My sister, Emily, walked into the living room, putting her nose where it didn't belong, as usual.

"First of all," she said. "'Crossing guard' has thirteen letters. And second of all, the answer is 'toenail.'"

My dad gave her a big smile.

"Thank you, honey," he said. Then he put down his puzzle and said, "We're going to the ninety-nine-cent store. Why don't you join us?"

"Noooooooooooo!" Frankie and Ashley and I cried all at once.

My dad gave us that look, the one that says *we're doing this my way.*

"Dad, Emily can't come," I tried to explain. "We have secret business to do that only the three of us can know about."

"Don't be ridiculous, Hank," my dad said. "We don't have secrets in this family. Emily, get your jacket."

Boy, was my dad ever wrong about not having secrets. We had one the size of Jupiter.

"Hank," Frankie whispered as we put on our jackets. "We can't buy the snake with Emily there."

"Don't worry about it, Frankie," I said with my most confident Zipzer attitude. "I have everything under control. Ashley will walk Emily to the other side of the store, and I'll pay for the snake. I got my wallet right here."

I patted my pocket. It was empty.

"Okay, so I don't have my wallet right here," I said.

I guess the old Zipzer attitude still needed a little work. I sure hoped I could fix it by the time we got to the store.

CHAPTER 6

"Ashley," I whispered as soon as we walked into the ninety-nine-cent store, "your job is to take Emily over there, to the art-supply section. That way, Frankie and I can pick out the snake without her seeing us."

"How am I supposed to do that?" Ashley asked. "You know Emily. She's going to want to go to the snake section."

"Tell her that you heard there's a new reptile sticker

book," I suggested. "Then go look for it. And take your time."

"Right-o, Captain Hank. I'm on it," Ashley said, giving me a salute.

I watched her go up to Emily and whisper something in her ear. Emily nodded happily, and the two of them set off for the other side of the store.

My dad had already found the crossword puzzle book section, and stuck his nose into one of the display books.

"Dad," I said. "Frankie and I will be in aisle three if you need us."

He was so involved in a puzzle that all he did was grunt.

We ran up and down the aisles, looking for the rubber-snake bin. It turned out it was actually in aisle three, between the canned artichokes and the tugboat toothbrushes, just like I remembered. We both dug into the bin, sorting through fat snakes, short ones, green ones . . . until we came across a black and orange and yellow striped one.

"Ginger!" I said. "Hey, nice to see you again."

"Don't tell me you and this snake have had pizza together," Frankie said, shooting me a look.

"Of course not. Everyone knows rubber snakes can't digest cheese."

Frankie burst out laughing. So did I. Unfortunately, we were a little too loud and attracted the attention of a certain almost-seven-year-old sister of mine. Out of the corner of my eye, I saw Emily hurrying over to our aisle, with Ashley following close behind.

"I'll distract her," I whispered to Frankie. "You go buy Ginger. I'll pay you back later."

With that, I spun around and raced down the aisle toward Emily.

"I want to see what's so funny!" she demanded.

I put myself right in front of her and tried to puff up my chest so she couldn't see around me. My chest doesn't puff up all that much, so instead, I started talking as fast as I could.

"Oh my gosh," I said, pointing to an entire shelf filled with baby shoes. "Look at those. Aren't they the cutest little things you've ever seen?"

Emily turned around and looked at the display of baby shoes. Ashley understood what I was doing and jumped right in.

"Oh, Emily, those baby shoes would look so perfect on your iguana," she said. "Of course, you'd have to buy two pairs."

"No problem," I said. "I've saved some allowance money. I'd like to get something for Katherine."

"Do you have a fever, Hank?" Emily asked. "I've never heard

you say anything nice about Katherine in my entire life."

"Well, it's time I did," I said. "She is one lovely lizard."

I took Emily by the hand and dragged her over to the baby shoes. I glanced at Frankie and saw that he was heading to the cash register, but he wasn't there yet. I had to stall for a little while longer. So I reached out and picked up two pairs of pink baby sneakers that had rainbow-colored ponies on them. I slipped each shoe onto one of my fingers and moved them up and down like they were dancing.

"Hi, Emily," I said in a high squeaky voice. "It's me, Katherine.

I'm a happy little iguana because
I'm dancing in these baby sneakers.
They're so soft, my claws feel like
they're walking on pillows."

Emily squinted at me like I
had lost my mind. I could see that
I was losing her attention, so I
had to step up my performance.
I started to twirl around, singing
a made-up song.

"I'm a dizzy little lizard, watch
me twirl," I sang, flapping my arms.
I must have flapped a little too
hard, because I lost my balance,
and my entire body crashed into
the stack of baby shoes. The next
thing I knew, the whole display
came tumbling down around me.
It was raining tiny sneakers.

"Hank!" Emily screamed. "Look what you did!"

All the shoppers around me stopped and stared. One of them had a stroller with twins in it. Both babies started to cry. Then a little boy came running over to the pile of shoes and dove into them. When he came up for air, a pair of baby blue running shoes was hanging off his ear. Another kid pointed and laughed, and then picked up a shoe and threw it in the air, just for fun. It landed right on my head.

Suddenly, there was a crackling noise on the loudspeaker.

"Clean up on aisle three," a man's voice said.

And before I knew it, two workers with brooms were at my side, sweeping the shoes into a pile. My dad had arrived, too, standing over me with his hands on his hips.

"Hank, why is it that trouble follows you wherever you go?" he said. "I can't leave you alone for two minutes."

"Actually, Mr. Z," Ashley said, "I think we were alone for at least three minutes, which is a new record for Hank."

"Ashley, I appreciate your attempt at humor, but this is not the time," my dad answered. "Look at this mess Hank has created."

Emily shook her head.

"I'm so sorry about my brother," she said to one of the workers.

I looked up to the front of the store and saw Frankie. He was holding a brown paper bag above his head.

"Frankie's got it," Ashley whispered in my ear.

I turned to the workers who were cleaning up the mess.

"Can I help you?" I asked.

"That's okay, kid. We got it. Accidents happen."

"I'm so sorry," I said. "Thanks for understanding." Then turning to Emily and my dad, I added, "Okay, let's go."

"But what about Katherine's sneakers?" Emily said.

I gave her a look like her brains had dropped onto the floor in the pile of shoes.

"Katherine?" I said. "Why would she need sneakers?"

As I ran down the aisle to meet Frankie, I high-fived myself. The plan didn't come off exactly as I had imagined it, but the snake was in the bag. Now all I had to do was learn how to pull it out.

CHAPTER 7

FOUR THINGS THAT HAPPENED WHEN FRANKIE TRIED TO TEACH ME THE MAGIC TRICK

BY HANK ZIPZER

1. I lost the velvet bag. (It's hard to pull something out of a bag when the bag itself has disappeared.)

2. I lost the chain of scarves. (I didn't actually lose them, but I used the blue one as a handkerchief when I sneezed. I gave it to my mom to wash, but I think the washing machine ate it.)

3. I accidentally spit out my bubble gum

and it got caught in my wizard beard. (Ashley had to cut it out, and now there's a hole the size of a silver-dollar pancake in my beard.)

4. I started to feel like getting an A in math would be easier than learning this trick. (And me getting an A in math is about as likely as a shark learning to ice-skate.)

By the way, in case you haven't figured this out already, learning the magic trick was not going well.

CHAPTER 8

"Hank," Frankie said to me. "This is the fifty-fifth time I've shown you this trick. You have to focus if you're ever going to learn it."

We were in the clubhouse, and I had been working with Frankie after school for four days. I was proud of myself just for having found the velvet bag and the scarves. I had stuffed them into my backpack. But now, every time I tried to pull the snake out of the bag, something went wrong.

"I'm really trying, Frankie, as hard as I can. I'm not messing up on purpose. I know I have to learn this trick, but I don't think I can."

"Time is running out," Ashley said. "It's already Thursday, and Emily's party is on Saturday."

"I'll never be able to do it by then," I said with a big sigh. "You're the magician, Frankie. Why don't you do it?"

"Hank, you can do this. I believe in you. If you give up now, you'll really feel bad."

"But if you get it," Ashley added, "you're going to feel good forever. You'll never forget what you did for Emily."

"But this is starting to really

freak me out," I said. "All Emily talks about is how many people have said yes to her party. Last night at dinner, she said there were seventeen for-sures and another ten maybes. Not one person said no."

"Okay," Frankie said, taking a deep breath. "Then let's stop wasting time. You're going to learn this."

I rolled up my wizard-robe sleeves and put on the sunglasses with the beard attached. I took a moment to scratch my nose, because the cotton balls tickled my nostrils.

"Hankster," Frankie said. "You have to become the Westside Wizard. And wizards don't scratch."

"Well, this one does."

"Fine," Frankie said. "Just go on with the trick."

"Okay," I began. "First, I lift my hand in the air. Then I drop it into the velvet bag until I find the secret pocket with the Velcro strip. Then, I say the magic word. What is it again, Frankie? Grapefruit?"

"No, *zengawii*. It doesn't even sound like grapefruit."

"*Zengawii!*" I repeated in my best wizardy voice.

I thought I felt the scarves tucked into the secret pocket. So far, so good. But when I pulled on the scarves, the whole bag flew across the room and landed smack in the middle of Mrs. Fink's laundry basket.

"That's it!" I yelled, pulling
off my beard and pointy wizard hat.
"I can't do this! I give up!"

"But, Hank—" Ashley began.

"No *but Hanks*," I told her.
"I'm so frustrated I could scream.
In fact, I think I will. *Aaaaaarrrrrrrr
rrrrgggggggggggggggggggg!*" I shouted
so loud I thought my tonsils were
going to fly out of my mouth.

"Hank, this isn't helping,"
Frankie said, covering his ears.

"If you keep this up, they're going to throw us out of here. Then you'll have no place to practice."

"I'm done practicing," I declared. "Done, done, and done. Oh, by the way, have I said the word *done*?"

"What about Emily and her party?" Ashley asked. "You promised her a snake. Are you just going to go back on your promise?"

"I'm going to solve this another way," I said. "The right way."

Before they could ask me another question, I hurried out of the clubhouse and headed for the elevator. Frankie and Ashley followed me up to my apartment. When I got inside, I picked up the phone and called Papa Pete.

"Hankie," he answered. "What are you up to, my boy?"

"Oh, about four foot three," I told him. He roared with laughter. That was our special joke.

"Papa Pete, can you help me?" I asked him. "I need you to come and pick me up. I have to visit a friend. I have a favor to ask him, and I don't want my mom and dad to know."

"You're not in any trouble, are you?" Papa Pete asked.

"No more than usual," I said.

Papa Pete is great because he doesn't bother you with too many questions, like most grown-ups do. He just tries to help.

"I'll be there soon," he said.

As I hung up the phone, Frankie and Ashley were staring at me.

"I'm not following this," Frankie said. "What friend? What favor?"

"His name is Ralph," I explained. "He's Ginger's owner. I'm going to ask him if he and Ginger can come to Emily's party."

"But didn't your dad say it was too expensive?" Ashley asked.

"That's where the favor part comes in. I'm going to ask if he can do it for two dollars and sixty-three cents. That's how much I have saved in my secret safe."

"Do you think Ralph will come for that?" Frankie asked. "It's not very much money, snake-wise."

"I don't know, Frankie," I said. "But like you just said, I can't let Emily down, so it's worth a try. Are you guys coming?"

"Oh, I wouldn't miss this," Ashley said.

"You're going to see Hank 'the Hurricane' Zipzer in action," I said. At that very moment, I was positive I could convince Ralph to come to Emily's party.

But a few minutes later, when the Hurricane died down, I wasn't so sure anymore.

CHAPTER 9

We took the bus to Ralph's apartment. It was downtown on 19th Street, above a discount suitcase store. We had to walk up three flights of stairs, slower than usual because Papa Pete had to rest on each landing. When we got to Ralph's door, the bell didn't work, so we knocked. And waited. And waited.

"Maybe he's not home," Ashley said.

"Oh, he's there," I answered.

"I called ahead and told him we were coming."

"How'd you get his number?"

"From his brochure in Emily's room. She sleeps with it under her pillow."

"Good planning, Hankie," Papa Pete said. "I like the way you're thinking ahead."

Suddenly, the door flew open and there was Ralph. Ginger was wrapped around his arm, and Boris, the blue-tailed skink, was relaxing on his shoulder. Ginger shot her tongue out at us, which made Frankie and Ashley take a giant step backward. Ralph laughed.

"You don't have to be afraid, kids," he said. "Ginger flicks her tongue to help her smell. It's how she knows you're here."

"Good thing I took a shower this morning," I said. "I wouldn't want to gross Ginger out."

Ralph threw his head back and laughed loudly. We all joined in.

"Our friend Hank is really funny," Frankie said.

"So I see," Ralph answered. "Come on in and meet the rest of the family."

The inside of Ralph's apartment was like a zoo, except you didn't have to pay to get in. There were glass cages everywhere, and inside each cage was some kind of reptile. Speedy, the giant tortoise, was sitting on

the couch watching **TV**. I think
it was an infomercial about an
exercise machine.

"Is **S**peedy interested in
working out?" I asked. "I bet it
would be hard to do sit-ups with
that shell in the way."

Ralph laughed again.

"You're on a roll, kid. Now,
what can I do for you? You said
you needed a favor."

I put on my biggest smile,

and took a deep breath so all the words would come out right.

"Ralph," I began. "Here is my problem: My sister, as annoying as she is, has only one wish in the whole wide world. And that wish is for you and Ginger to come to her birthday party. It's this Saturday at noon."

"I remember talking about this with your family at the street fair, but your parents never called," Ralph said.

"That's why I'm here. I think a personal invitation is always best. Don't you think so, Papa Pete?"

"Personal is good," Papa Pete agreed.

"Ralph," I said, "I'm going to

give you three reasons why you
have to come to Emily's party.
One: The birthday cake will be so
delicious it'll make your socks go
up and down. Two: You will make
an almost-seven-year-old girl's
dream come true. And three: I have
here in my pocket two dollars and
sixty-three cents . . . and it's all
yours."

I paused and gave him my best
upper and lower
teeth grin.

He was quiet for a minute.
I took that as a good sign. I
flashed Frankie and Ashley a
confident grin. *Yup, this was Hank
"the Hurricane" Zipzer in action,*
I thought. *Hank, you have done
a good job here. I think you've
saved the day.*

Ralph walked over to his dusty
desk and pulled out a spiral
notebook with a picture of two
snakes on the cover. I think they
were hugging, but without arms.
He brought the notebook over to
me and opened it to a page with
a calendar on it.

"Hank, I am so sorry," he said.
"But as you can see on this
calendar, I am busy every day for

the next three weekends. This Saturday, Ginger and I have an appearance at the Central Park Zoo. And then we're performing at Tiffany Nelson's birthday party on Park Avenue."

"But, Ralph," I said, "you know how much you love your reptiles. There is only one other person on the planet who feels the way you do about them—my sister. If you come to her party, it will be the best birthday present I could ever give her. Forever."

You're not going to believe this, but when I said those words, I actually felt a lump in my throat, the kind you get before you cry. I meant every word I was saying.

Ralph reached out and put his hand on my shoulder, which brought Ginger dangerously close to my nose.

"Hank," he said, "I think you're a wonderful young man and a great big brother. But there is nothing I can do. Saturday is just completely booked. I'm so sorry."

I felt another hand on my shoulder. It was Papa Pete.

"Hank, you tried your best," he said. "But business is business, and Ralph can't do it. So thank the kind man and let's be on our way. We've taken up enough of his time."

I shook hands with Ralph and
tried to smile at Ginger. I didn't
smile at Boris, but he didn't
seem to mind. I guess skinks are
like that.

As we left, I heard Ashley call out, "By the way, Ralph, Hank lives at Two Hundred Ten West Seventy-Eighth Street, in case anything, anything, anything changes."

"That's between Broadway and Amsterdam," Frankie added.

I really appreciated that both of my friends were still trying their best, even when there seemed to be no hope. As for me, all I was thinking was that I had one more day to learn that trick.

Right. Somebody tell that to my brain.

CHAPTER 10

That day and the next,
I spent every spare minute in the
clubhouse with Frankie and Ashley,
going over the magic trick again
and again. Finally, on Friday night
at exactly 8:17 p.m., I got it right.
And not only that, I got it right
three times in a row. Costume on.
Hand into velvet bag. Find secret
pocket. Pull out handkerchief
chain. Say *zengawii* and produce
rubber snake. Wave hands in the
air and take a bow. I did it all.

"See, Zip," Frankie said. "I told you that if you kept your mind on it, you could do it. And you did it!"

"You are now officially the Westside Wizard," Ashley added. "There's only one thing left to do. Hand over your beard."

"Excuse me," I said in my wizardy voice. "It took me a long time to grow this."

"Now isn't the time to be cute, Hank," Ashley said. "I have to fill that hole with another cotton ball. You're going to have twenty-five kids looking at you tomorrow. That's fifty eyeballs."

While Ashley glued a cotton ball onto my beard, Frankie and I

opened a package of chocolate-
chip cookies I had brought down
to the clubhouse with me. As
I chewed my cookie, I couldn't
stop a smile from spreading
across my face.

"Dude, don't smile so wide
when you're eating," Frankie said.
"I can see chocolate chunks stuck
to your teeth."

"I can't help it, Frankie. I just
feel so proud for learning something
I thought I could never do."

"You're going to be great," Ashley said. "Those little kids will be amazed. And Emily is going to be so happy, she won't know what to say."

"Oh, that will never happen. She hasn't stopped talking about it all week."

The last thing Ashley, Frankie, and I did that night was carefully pack the costume into a shopping bag so I could sneak it back into the apartment without Emily seeing it. We arranged to meet in our clubhouse at a few minutes before noon the next morning.

When I got back to the apartment, Emily and my mom were busy decorating the living room for

the party. My mom was blowing up
balloons, and Emily was using her
colored markers to draw pictures
of snakes and lizards on them.
She wasn't a bad artist. One of
her drawings actually looked like
Boris the blue-tailed skink.

Without even looking up, Emily said, "What's in the bag, Hank?"

I swear that girl has eyes glued to the side of her head.

"Nothing," I answered, hurrying into my room and closing the door.

My mom followed me into my room.

"Hank," she said. "I know what you're up to. Frankie's mom and I have been talking, and I know that you're planning a surprise for Emily."

"You didn't say anything to Emily, did you?"

"Of course not. I wouldn't spoil your plan. But I just

want to warn you: It's not easy to entertain twenty–five first-graders. I hope you know what you're doing."

"Don't you worry, Mom. The wizard is with us."

"Well then, good luck to you, honey. Oh, I mean, to *him*."

As my mom walked out the door, Emily stuck her head in.

"Have you checked with the wizard lately?" she asked.

"I can't wait to meet him. I've never met a real wizard before."

"Me neither," I said.

Emily looked surprised.

"Wait a minute, Hank. I thought you said you knew him."

There it was . . . my foot in my mouth. Actually, both my feet were in there. When would I learn to keep my big mouth shut?

"Oh . . . yeah . . . ," I stammered. "Of course I know him. I was just joking with you, Emily. A little birthday-party humor."

"Well, I don't think it's funny.

I've been looking forward to this all week. It's not nice to tease me the night before the best day of my life."

The last thing I saw was her braids whip through the air as she turned around and slammed the door shut.

Emily's words rang in my ears. The best day of her life. Wow, she wasn't kidding around about this wizard thing. My stomach did a flip-flop. As I looked at the paper bag with my wizard costume shoved inside, I realized that I had better come through, or I was going to have one sad sister on my hands.

CHAPTER 11

The next day was party day. The sun decided to come out bright and clear. Emily took it as a sign.

"You see," she said at breakfast. "Even the sun is happy that it's my birthday."

"I bet the Westside Wizard made the sun come out," I said, popping the rest of my buttered toast in my mouth.

"Do you really think so, Hank?" she asked, her eyes wide with excitement.

"He must have incredible powers."

"Of course he does." I gulped. "Let's just hope he brings them all with him today."

I got up and hurried into my room. I practiced the trick for one hour straight. I got it right about half of the time. That was better than getting it right none of the time. But not as good as getting it right all of the time. At a few minutes before noon, I took my costume and headed for the clubhouse.

Our living room was already filling up with kids.

Frankie and Ashley were waiting for me at the elevator in the basement.

"It's crazy up there in my living room," I told them. "It's swarming with first-graders. They're like bees . . . but without stingers."

Frankie and Ashley helped me into my costume. Ashley adjusted my beard and added more tape to make sure it held on to the sunglasses.

"Okay, you're ready," Frankie said, checking me up and down.

We headed to the elevator. I was pretty nervous.

"I'm going to go out there first and get all those wild kids to sit down," Frankie said calmly. "Ashley will wait by the front door of your apartment."

I nodded, trying to listen carefully.

Frankie continued. "When she hears me say *Make some noise for the Westside Wizard,* she'll open the door. That's when you come in and work your way through the crowd. Be sure not to step on any kids while you're at it."

"Yeah," Ashley agreed, "because if you do, they'll kick you. Trust me, I know."

When the elevator doors opened on the tenth floor,

I could feel my heart beating
fast under my heavy wizard coat.

"I hope this goes okay,"
I whispered to Ashley.

"You did the trick perfectly
last night," she reminded me.
"Just do everything you practiced
and it will be fine."

Frankie went into the living
room. From the hall, I could hear
his introduction. The kids applauded
and cheered. Ashley opened the
door for me. This was it. Showtime.

I walked into the living room,
holding my arms high up in the air.

"Behold, all you tiny tots,"
I called out in my best wizard
voice. "The Westside Wizard
has arrived."

From the corner of my eye,
I could see Papa Pete, leaning
against the wall. He winked. I
wondered how he knew it was me.

As I walked by the kids, I could
hear lots of oohs and ahhs coming
from their direction. Hey, this was
working! At least it was until one
little boy with a mouthful of jelly
beans reached up and tugged on
my coat. I whirled around and gave
him the stare of a lifetime.

"What is your name, child?"
I boomed.

"Eugie Pasos," he said.

"Well, Eugie, the wizard does
not like to be touched," I growled.
"Nor does his coat!"

Eugie actually looked kind of

scared, and leaned back away from me. I was feeling the wizard power, and it felt good.

When I reached the front of the crowd, I turned slowly to face them.

"Is there an Emily Zipzer here?" I half-shouted.

Emily was sitting cross-legged in the front row, holding Cheerio in her lap. He is such a long wiener dog that even when curled up, his hind legs were hanging over on the rug.

When he saw me, Cheerio sniffed the air and let out a little whimper. I looked away, hoping he wouldn't recognize me.

Emily put Cheerio down and jumped up to face me.

"Here I am, Oh Great Wizard," she said. "Did you bring a snake for me?"

"Why, yes I did," I called out. "But let me warn you, folks. You all must stay seated and remain quiet. Snakes have very sensitive ears."

"No, they don't," Emily shot back. "They hear through their bones."

Wouldn't you know it, my know-it-all sister chose this

moment to give everybody a reptile lesson.

"You are correct, Birthday Girl," I said. "Now, please sit down. And hold your dog tightly. Frankie, will you please hand me the magic snake bag? Very carefully!"

Frankie handed me the bag. I turned it inside out and showed the kids that it was completely empty. No one could see the Velcro pocket.

"Observe that there is nothing in this bag but air," I said. I pushed the wizard coat sleeves up as high as they could go. "And notice also that there is nothing up my sleeves," I added.

"Except for very skinny arms," Eugie Pasos shouted out. He should talk. His arms were so skinny, they looked like  pencils without erasers.

"Silence, please. Keep your eyes focused on the bag and prepare to be amazed. I will now say the magic word. Are you ready?"

"Yes!" Emily yelled. And the other kids joined in. "Snake, snake, snake," they chanted. Even Cheerio barked in time to their chant.

"Silence!" I shouted. A hush fell over the crowd. I waved one hand

wildly over the opening of the bag.
In my best wizard voice, I called
out "*Zengawii*! *Zengawii*!" I said
it a second time just in case the
first time didn't work.

Then I reached into the bag
and found the Velcro pocket.
Yes! So far, so good. My fingers
fumbled around and found the
handkerchief chain. All I needed
now was one good tug, and it
would come flying out with the
rubber snake attached.

"*Zengawii*!" I hollered one
more time, just for fun. Grabbing
the end of the handkerchief
between my thumb and my pointer
finger, I yanked. And unbelievable
as it may seem, the colorful

handkerchiefs came flying out of
the bag, dragging the rubber snake
behind.

I grabbed the snake and spun
it around over my head so no
one could tell it was rubber. And
then I waited for the sound of the
applause.

It never came.

CHAPTER 12

As I twirled the snake above
my head, Cheerio leaped off
Emily's lap and flew through the
air toward my beard. Grabbing
the end with his mouth, he pulled
on it like a play toy. I think he
thought it was Mousie, his white
furry toy that I throw across the
room for him to catch. Anyway,
he yanked on it with all his might.

"Cheerio, get down," I said in
my wizard voice.

"How do you know my

dog's name?" Emily called out.

Oops.

"The wizard knows all," I said, covering my mistake.

I should have known that Cheerio would recognized my scent. He sniffed the air, his little brown nose working as hard as it could. He was so glad to see me, he jumped up even higher, getting a big hunk of my beard in his mouth. He tugged and growled at it, just like we do when we wrestle with Mousie.

I tried desperately to hold on to my beard. But Cheerio thought we were playing, and pulled even harder. With one mighty tug, he yanked the entire beard off my face, pulling the sunglasses off

along with it.
I watched in horror
as the beard and
sunglasses went
flying through
the air.

I just stood there
with my own face hanging out.
All the little kids burst into wild
laughter.

Ashley took off after my beard,
which was still stuck in Cheerio's
mouth. Frankie, good friend that
he is, tried to save the day.

"As you can see, kids, the
wizard has magical powers and
can change his face to look like
anybody."

"That's not anybody!" Emily

screamed. "It's just my goofball brother, Hank."

"Okay," I said. "It is me. But I still made a snake appear, didn't I? And how cool is that! Happy birthday, sis."

"You call that a snake?" Emily cried. "I call that a thing that you got on sale at the ninety-nine-cent store."

All the kids were howling with laughter now, but not Emily. She looked like she was going to cry.

"Hey, Emily," Eugie called out. "You promised us a real snake, not some stupid rubber thing."

Emily stood up and started to run to her bedroom. My mom caught her halfway.

"Well, we still have delicious cake, everyone," she said, trying extra hard to be cheerful. "Emily, come on. Let's light the candles."

She put her arm around Emily and gently led her back to the dining-room table, where the cake was waiting. It was shaped like a snake, and when Emily saw it, she almost burst into tears again.

"I wish that was real," she said. "I'd have it eat Hank."

Just then, the doorbell rang. My dad made his way across the living room to answer it while Papa Pete helped my mom light the candles.

"Before you blow out the candles, make a wish, sweetie," she said.

"I wish Ginger the snake was here," Emily said.

"She is," a voice rang out. Everyone's head spun around at the same time and we saw Ralph being led into the dining room by my dad. Ginger was wrapped around his arm, and Boris the skink was happily riding on his shoulder.

Everyone in the room let out a
gasp, the loudest one coming from
my sister, Emily.

"Ginger!" she screamed, dashing
over to Ralph and reaching out
to pet Ginger gently on her head.
"I can't believe you came. Daddy,
thank you so much!"

"I didn't do anything," my dad said.

"Neither did I," my mom added.

"Me neither," Papa Pete said.

"It was your big brother, little lady," Ralph said. "He came all the way to my apartment to invite me here today."

"But you said you couldn't make it," I said to Ralph.

"I left the other party early so I could pay Emily a visit," Ralph answered.

"Why?" I asked him. I didn't understand.

Ralph took off his big brown hat and turned to Emily. "I was mighty impressed with your brother, Hank," he said to her.

"He wanted this to be the best birthday you ever had. When I was your age . . . hey, even now . . . I wish I'd had a brother like that. Hank really cares about you. And I just couldn't say no to him."

Emily turned around slowly and looked me right in the eyes.

"You did this for me?" she whispered.

I just shrugged.

"He did," Frankie said. "We were there."

What happened next was truly amazing in a creepy kind of way. Emily threw both her arms around me and squeezed me so hard, my eyes popped out a little bit.

"I love you, Hank," she said.

I felt like she was waiting for me to say "I love you" back. Luckily I didn't have to because just at that moment, Ginger decided to slither off Ralph's arm and rest her head on Emily's head.

"And Ginger loves you," Ralph said. "I think she's saying she wants to do a show. How about it, kids?"

Everyone cheered and we all went into the living room. If Ginger was tired from the other party, she sure didn't show it. She let each kid pet her and didn't even hiss once. At the end of the show, Emily got to hold Ginger and smile into her snakey eyes. I stood next to Papa Pete as he took pictures of Emily's beaming face. Then he turned to me and put a hand on my shoulder.

"She is one happy girl," Papa Pete said. "You did a good thing, Hankie."

"The good thing is that Ralph

showed up," I said. "My magic trick was a total flop."

"Don't you believe that," Papa Pete said. "You have the real magic—and that is your great big caring heart. No magic trick can ever beat that."

I have to say, it did feel really good to have helped Emily get the birthday party of her dreams. I felt proud and happy.

That is, until Ginger decided to give me a kiss! Trust me, folks. That was a real party ender.

CHAPTER 13
THREE THINGS I'D WANT AT THE BIRTHDAY PARTY OF MY DREAMS
BY HANK ZIPZER

1. My very own personal robot named Gordon
2. A trampoline made out of pepperoni pizza
3. A roller coaster with a loop in my living room

I just thought of this too: a candy-bar cake.

Oh, and you're all invited!!!!!!!